Henr

The Mentor, Russian Music

outlook

Henry T. Finck

The Mentor, Russian Music

1st Edition | ISBN: 978-3-75234-823-1

Place of Publication: Frankfurt am Main, Germany

Year of Publication: 2020

Outlook Verlag GmbH, Germany.

Reproduction of the original.

THE
MENTOR

RUSSIAN MUSIC

By HENRY T. FINCK

Several Natural Questions

Q.—How big is Russia, and what is its population?

A.—The area of Russia exceeds 8,660,000 square miles, or one-sixth o land surface of the earth. Its population is over 150,000,000—or at leas before the war.

Q.—How many famous Russian composers are there?

A.—Less than a dozen.

Q.—How old is Russian music?

A.—Less than 150 years. Catherine the Great (1761-1796) was one of encourage national music in Russia. Before her time the music performe was imported, and was largely Italian. Catherine caused productions o Russian composers. She supplied the libretto for one opera.

Q.—What is the origin of Russian music?

A.—Both the music and literature of Russia had a common origi inspiration. The form and spirit of the music and literature were draw legends and primitive songs of the people.

Q.—When did music in Russia become, in a real sense, national?

A.—Not until the first part of the nineteenth century. Composers had bee fifty years to establish a national movement in music, but it was not until th Glinka and his opera, "A Life for the Czar," in 1836, that the Russian scho can be said to have been inaugurated.

Q.—Why were music and literature so late in coming to this great nation?

A.—On account of physical and human conditions. Russia is and has and absolute monarchy, consisting of millions of people held in sub ignorance, and with only a few great centers of civilization. Petrograd h years a city of brilliant cultivation, but in contrast to that there are count villages, and farms in which dwell millions of poor and ignorant people within the last century that Russia has wakened to a national consciousness to shake off the grim, feudal conditions of the Middle Ages. In this new e of music is first heard as a national expression.

MICHAL IVANOVICH GLINKA

Michal Ivanovich Glinka

Michal Ivanovich Glinka at an early age showed that he possessed two characteristics that were to have a very important bearing on his whole life— an extremely nervous disposition and a lively aptitude for music. His grandmother, who was responsible for his early upbringing and who was an invalid herself, encouraged the first; while his father stimulated in the boy the second. Glinka, mollycoddled from childhood, never wholly succeeded in throwing off an inherited brooding tendency; but he became a wonderful composer and musician.

Glinka was born on June 2, 1803, at Novospassky, a little village in Russia. His father was a retired army officer and not particularly well off, but his mother's brother was fairly wealthy, and often when the Glinkas had an entertainment this brother lent them a small private band which he kept up. It was to this early association with music of the best class that young Glinka owed the development of his taste.

He spent his earliest years at home, but when he was thirteen he went to a boarding school in Petrograd, where he remained for five years, carefully studying music. It was in 1822, when he was only seventeen, that he composed his first music—one of his five waltzes for the piano. During these school years he paid attention to the other branches of education also, learning Latin, French, German, English and Persian, and working hard at the study of geography and zoölogy.

Glinka had a nervous breakdown in 1823, and he made a tour of the Caucasus, taking a cure in the waters there. On his return home he worked hard at his music, although as he had not then decided to devote his life to a musical career, his studies were somewhat intermittent. He went to Petrograd and took a position in the government department; but in 1828 his family gave him an allowance and he decided to devote himself to music alone. While at Petrograd he made many friends. However, he saw that a round of pleasure did not aid him in his music, so in 1830 he began his thorough musical education, leaving Russia for Italy, where he stayed for three years studying the works of old and modern Italian masters. His training as a composer was finally finished in Berlin.

Glinka returned to Russia in 1833, and was soon the center of an intellectual circle at Petrograd. It was one of these friends, Joukovsky, the poet, who suggested that Glinka compose an opera on the subject of the heroic patriotic deeds of the Russian hero, Ivan Soussanin. Baron de Rosen wrote the libretto for this work, which was called "A Life for the Czar," and which was first performed on November 27, 1836.

The plot of this opera was based on the following story: In 1613 the Poles invaded Russia and attempted to assassinate the newly elected Czar, Michael Romanoff. The Polish leaders, however, did not know where to find the Czar. Without letting him know who they were, they asked a peasant, Ivan Soussanin, to guide them to the monarch. Ivan, however, suspecting their designs, sent his adopted son to warn the Czar, and himself led the Poles to the depths of a forest from which they could not possibly find their way. The Poles, when they saw that they had been deceived, killed Soussanin.

This opera was the turning point in Glinka's life. It was a great success, and in a way became the basis of a Russian school of national music. The opera enjoyed extraordinary popularity. In December, 1879, it reached its 500th performance, and in November, 1886, a special production was given, not only at Petrograd, but in every Russian town that had a theater, in celebration of the 50th anniversary of its first performance. It was presented at two theaters in Moscow at the same time.

Glinka had married in 1835, but misunderstandings arose which finally ended in a separation some time afterward.

His second opera, "Ruslan and Ludmilla," did not appear until 1842. It did not appeal to the popular taste and was a dismal failure. Glinka thought that it was superior to his first, and he was bitterly disappointed at its failure.

In 1845 he made his first visit to Paris, and later he went to Spain. After two years in that country he returned to Russia, where he spent the winter at his home, and then went to Warsaw, remaining there for three years. In 1852 Glinka started for France, paying another visit to Berlin on the way. When, however, war broke out in the Crimea in 1854, he returned to Petrograd. While there he became interested in church music. In order to study this type of music he went to Berlin in 1856. This was his last journey. Early in January, 1857, the composer Meyerbeer arranged a special concert devoted to Glinka's works. On leaving the hall the Russian contracted a chill. He died on February 15, 1857. Glinka was buried in Berlin. Three months later, however, his body was taken to its present resting place in Petrograd. A monument was erected to his memory there in 1906.

PREPARED BY THE EDITORIAL STAFF OF THE MENTOR ASSOCIATION
ILLUSTRATION FOR THE MENTOR, VOL. 4, No. 18, SERIAL No. 118

ANTON RUBINSTEIN

Anton Rubinstein

TWO

There has been a curious uncertainty as to the date of Anton Rubinstein's birth. He was born on November 28, 1829, but due to a lapse of memory on the part of his mother, he always celebrated his birthday on the 30th of November. He was the son of a Jewish pencil manufacturer at Wechwotynetz, Russia, who later went to Moscow. In his autobiography Rubinstein tells of this migration: "My earliest recollections are of a journey to Moscow in a roomy covered wagon, undertaken by the three families, with all the children and servants,—nothing less than a tribal migration. We reached the city and crossed the Pokròvski bridge. Here we hired a large house belonging to a certain Madame Pozniakòv; it was surrounded by trees and stood near a pond beyond the river Iowza. This was in 1834 and 1835."

The mother of Rubinstein was an excellent musician, and she gave the young boy his first music lessons. In addition he had as a teacher a master of the piano named Alexander Villoing. To the end of his life Rubinstein declared that he had never met a better master.

When he was only ten years old Rubinstein made his first public appearance as a performer, playing in a theater at Moscow. Two years later he went to Paris, and roused the admiration of Liszt and Chopin by his playing.

After this Rubinstein traveled for some time in Holland, Germany and Scandinavia. In 1842 he reached England, where he made his first appearance, on May 20th. He made a brief visit to Moscow in 1843, and two years later went with his family to Berlin, in order to finish his musical education. There he made friends with Mendelssohn.

Then Rubinstein's father died suddenly. His mother and brother were forced to return to Moscow. Anton went to Vienna to earn a living. For nearly two years more he studied hard there, and then went on two concert tours through Hungary. The Revolution broke out in Vienna and prevented his return to that city, so he went to Petrograd, where he studied, composed and lived pleasantly for the next few years.

About this time he came near being exiled to Siberia through an unfortunate error of the police. He was saved from this by his patroness, the Grand Duchess Helene.

He composed several operas during the next few years; and he visited Hamburg and Leipzig and then went on to London, arriving there for the second time in 1857. He remained there for a short time and reappeared the following year, in the meantime having been appointed concert director of the Royal Russian Musical Society. In 1862 he helped to found the Conservatory at Petrograd. Of this he was director until 1867.

Rubinstein then traveled for some years, visiting America in 1872—a tour which brought him $40,000. So popular was his playing that he was afterward offered $125,000 for fifty concerts; but he could not overcome his dread of the sea voyage. He returned to Russia from America, and after a short rest continued his concert tours. For the remaining years of his life he lived in turn at Petrograd, Berlin, and Dresden, devoting his time to concerts, teaching, and to composition. In 1885 he began a series of historical recitals, which he gave in most of the chief European capitals. Rubinstein died near Petrograd on November 20, 1894.

PREPARED BY THE EDITORIAL STAFF OF THE MENTOR ASSOCIATION
ILLUSTRATION FOR THE MENTOR, VOL. 4, No. 18, SERIAL No. 118
COPYRIGHT, 1916, BY THE MENTOR ASSOCIATION, INC.

MODESTE PETROVICH MOUSSORGSKY

Modeste Petrovich Moussorgsky

THREE

Moussorgsky's artistic creed might be summed up in one sentence—he was devoted absolutely to the principle of "art for *life's* sake." This is quite the opposite of "Art for art's sake." Moussorgsky looked on musical art not as an end in itself, but as a means of vital expression. He was a full-blooded realist, and his music throbs with life.

Modeste Petrovich Moussorgsky was born on the estate of his father at Karevo on March 28, 1839. His father was a man of moderate means, and the boy spent his first ten years in the country and in close touch with the peasants. This early environment inspired his later feelings of sympathy with the land and its people. Long before he could play the piano he tried to reproduce songs that he heard among the peasants. His mother was pleased at this, and began to give him lessons on the piano when he was still a young child. At the age of seven he was able to play some of the smaller pieces of Liszt. Sometimes he even improvised musical settings for the fairy tales that his nurse told him.

In 1849 Moussorgsky and his brother were taken to Petrograd, where they were entered in the military cadet school, for the boy was intended for the army. At the same time, however, his parents allowed him to pursue his musical education. Moussorgsky's father died in 1853, and three years later the youth entered his regiment. It was in 1857 that he began to have a distaste for his military duties, and two years later he resigned from the army. During the summer following his resignation, however, he was unable to do any work with his music, as he was taken sick with nervous trouble. Also from the time he left the army he was never free from financial embarrassments.

Moussorgsky went to Petrograd, and he and five friends formed themselves into an intellectual circle. He soon, however, began to feel the pinch of poverty and was obliged to do some work of translation. Later he even took a small government position. His mother died in 1865, and he wrote a song at the time which is now regarded as one of his finest works. Toward the middle of this year he was once more attacked by his nervous trouble. It was necessary for him to give up his position and to go to live in the country. He improved gradually, and during the next two years he wrote some songs which later attracted some attention. Most of the year 1868 was spent in the country. In the fall of this year he returned to Petrograd. He secured another position, this one in the Ministry of the Interior. This left him with some leisure, which he employed with his music. About this time he began to work on the music of his opera, "Boris Godounov," based on the work of the dramatist Pushkin. This was first produced in Petrograd on January 24, 1874. Shortly after he began to work on "Khovantchina," another opera, which had its first complete public performance in 1885 at Petrograd.

Shortly after the production of "Boris Godounov," Moussorgsky began to devote himself to the composition of songs, among which was the song, "Without Sunlight," and the "Songs and Dances of Death."

Then Moussorgsky began to enter into a mental and physical decline. He was low in funds, for the small salary derived from his government position was insufficient for his needs. He began to play accompaniments at concerts, but very little work of this kind was obtainable. In 1879 he made a long concert tour in South Russia with Madam Leonoff, a singer of repute. This was very successful. He did very little work during the following winter; his health grew worse, and he was forced to give up his government appointment. He lived for a time in the country. At last it was necessary for him to enter the military hospital at Petrograd, where he died on March 28, 1881. He was buried in the Alexander Nevsky cemetery. Some years later a few friends and admirers erected a monument over his grave.

PREPARED BY THE EDITORIAL STAFF OF THE MENTOR ASSOCIATION
ILLUSTRATION FOR THE MENTOR, VOL. 4, No. 18, SERIAL No. 118
COPYRIGHT, 1916, BY THE MENTOR ASSOCIATION, INC.

PETER ILICH TCHAIKOVSKY

FOUR

Peter Ilich Tchaikovsky

Peter Ilich Tchaikovsky in the first part of his life held an office in the Ministry of Justice at Petrograd. While he was an excellent amateur performer, he did not think seriously enough of his musical ability to consider music as a career. It was Anton Rubinstein who induced him to take up music as a profession.

Tchaikovsky was born at Votkinsk, Russia, on May 7, 1840. He was the son of a mining engineer, who shortly after Peter was born removed to Petrograd. The boy picked up a smattering of musical knowledge as a law student. Then when he was twenty-two, Rubinstein, the director of the conservatory at Petrograd, persuaded him to enter it as a pupil. Tchaikovsky, therefore, resigned his position in the Ministry of Justice and took up the study of composition, harmony, and counterpoint. Four years later, on leaving the conservatory, he won the prize, a silver medal, for his cantata on Schiller's "Ode to Joy."

In 1866 Tchaikovsky became professor of the history and theory of music at the Moscow Conservatory, which had just then been founded by Nicholas Rubinstein, a brother of Anton. For the next twelve years he was practically first chief of this conservatory, since Serov, whom he succeeded, never took up his appointment. While serving in that capacity he wrote text books and made translations of others into Russian.

At Moscow Tchaikovsky met Ostrovsky, who wrote for him his first operatic libretto, "The Voyevoda." The Russian Musical Society rejected a concert overture by Tchaikovsky, written at the suggestion of Rubinstein. In 1867 Tchaikovsky made an unsuccessful début as a conductor. His star was not yet in the ascendant, for in 1869 his opera, "The Voyevoda," lived for only ten performances. Tchaikovsky later destroyed the score of this work. The following year his operatic production, "Undine," was rejected. In 1873, at Moscow, his incidental music to the "Snow Queen" proved a failure. During all this time the composer was busy on a cantata, an opera and a text book of harmony, the last of which was adopted by the authorities of the Moscow Conservatory. He was also music critic for two journals.

Tchaikovsky competed for the best musical setting for Polovsky's "Wakula the Smith" in a competition, and won the first two prizes. On the production of this in Petrograd, in November, 1876, however, only a small measure of success was gained. A greater success came to the composer with the production of the "Oprischnik." From 1878 on he devoted himself exclusively to composition.

On July 6, 1877, Tchaikovsky married. It was a most unfortunate match and rapidly developed into a catastrophe. Tchaikovsky had too much temperament—result, many stormy scenes. A separation occurred in October. Tchaikovsky became morose, and finally left Moscow to make his home in Petrograd. He fell ill there and attempted to commit suicide by standing up to his chin in the river during a cold period. He had hoped to die from exposure, but his brother's tender care saved his life.

Tchaikovsky had begun work on the opera, "Eugen Onegin," in 1877. This work was produced at the Moscow Conservatory in March, 1879, and it was then that real success first came to him.

In the meanwhile, however, Tchaikovsky went to Clarens to recuperate from his illness. He remained abroad for several months, visiting Italy and Switzerland, and moving restlessly from one place to another.

In 1878 he accepted the post of director of the Russian Musical Department at the Paris Exhibition. He resigned this later on. In 1879 he wrote his "Maid of Orleans," which was produced in 1880. During the next five years he continued his travels, working all the time at composition. For some time he lived in retirement at Klin, where his generosity to the poor made him much loved. In 1888 and 1889 he appeared at the London Philharmonic concerts. He also visited America, conducting his own compositions in New York City at the opening of Carnegie Hall in 1891. In 1893 Cambridge University made him a doctor of music. In the same year he died from an attack of cholera at Petrograd, on November 6.

PREPARED BY THE EDITORIAL STAFF OF THE MENTOR ASSOCIATION
ILLUSTRATION FOR THE MENTOR, VOL. 4, No. 18, SERIAL No. 118
COPYRIGHT, 1916, BY THE MENTOR ASSOCIATION, INC.

NICHOLAS ANDREIEVICH RIMSKY-KORSAKOV

Nicholas Andreievich Rimsky-Korsakov

FIVE

Rimsky-Korsakov was one of the many Russian composers who took up a musical career after a future had been planned along the line of some other work. In his case the Navy lost where music gained. Nicholas Andreievich Rimsky-Korsakov was born March 18, 1844, at Tikhvin, Russia. He had the good fortune to spend his early life in the country, and at the same time to hear from infancy the best music. On the estate of his father were four Jews, who formed a little band. This band supplied music at all social functions that took place at the Korsakov home. He began to study the piano when he was six years old, and three years later he was improvising.

The boy's parents, although they were glad to have him study music, planned a naval career for him. When he was twelve years old, in 1856, he was sent to the Petrograd Naval College. While studying there, however, he continued his music. In 1861 he began to take his musical studies very seriously. The following year, however, he had to conclude his naval education with a three years' cruise in foreign waters. When this cruise was over, in 1865, a symphony that he had composed had its first performance. This symphony bears the distinction of being the first musical work in that form by a Russian composer.

In 1866 began Korsakov's friendship with Moussorgsky, which lasted until the latter's death in 1881. From then on, for the next few years, he worked hard at musical composition. It was during this time that he first began to turn his attention to opera, of which "Pskovitianka," begun in 1870, was the first. In 1871 Rimsky-Korsakov was appointed a professor in the Conservatory at Petrograd. Two years later he decided to sever his connection with the Navy altogether. This year also saw the beginning of his collection of folk songs, which were published in 1877. The year before this, Korsakov had married. His wife was Nadejda Pourgold, the talented Russian pianist.

In 1874 the composer was made director of the Free School of Music at Petrograd, which position he filled until 1881. His second opera, "A Night in May," was finished in 1878. He began another opera, "The Snow Maiden," two years later. His operas, however, always attracted less attention abroad than his symphonies.

In 1883 he was appointed assistant director of the Imperial Chapel at Petrograd. This post was held by him for eleven years. Two years later he was offered the directorship of the Conservatory in Moscow, but he declined it. In 1886 he became director of the Russian symphony concerts. Three years later he appeared in Paris and conducted two concerts. He was enthusiastically received, and entertained at a banquet.

In 1894 Rimsky-Korsakov gave up the assistant directorship of the Imperial Chapel. He was now at work upon an opera in which the element of humor predominated. This was "Christmas Eve Revels." It was produced at the Maryinsky Theater in Petrograd in 1895. Korsakov continued to work at opera, producing, among others, "Sadko," "The Czar's Betrothed," "The Tale of Czar Saltan," "Servilia," "Kostchei the Deathless," "Pan Voyvoda," and "Kitej." His last opera, "The Golden Cock," was censored during the interval between its composition and the composer's death. It was not until May, 1910, that it was produced at Moscow. It is supposed that chagrin at the fate of this opera contributed to the suddenness of Rimsky-Korsakov's death, which occurred on June 20, 1908.

"In him we see," says one writer, "the Russian who, though not by any means satisfied with Russia as he finds it, does not set himself to hurl a series of passionate but ineffective indictments against things as they are, but who raises an ideal and does his utmost to show how best that ideal may be attained."

PREPARED BY THE EDITORIAL STAFF OF THE MENTOR ASSOCIATION
ILLUSTRATION FOR THE MENTOR, VOL. 4, No. 18, SERIAL No. 118

IGOR STRAVINSKY

Igor Stravinsky

Igor Stravinsky was a pupil of Rimsky-Korsakov. One day the young composer played for his teacher a few bars of the music of one of his ballets. The older man halted him suddenly: "Look here," said he. "Stop playing that horrid thing; otherwise I might begin to enjoy it!" This ballet was one of the works that made Stravinsky famous. Igor Stravinsky was born on June 17, 1882, at Oranienbaum, near Petrograd, Russia. The date of his birth has been disputed, but this date is the one given by Stravinsky himself. He was the son of Fedor Ignatievich Stravinsky, the celebrated singer who was associated with the Imperial (Maryinsky) Theater in Petrograd. Igor was destined to study law, but at the age of nine he was already giving proofs of a natural musical bent; and in particular he showed an aptitude for piano playing. To the study of this instrument he devoted a great deal of time, under the instruction of a pupil of Rubinstein.

In 1902, when Stravinsky was twenty years old, he met Rimsky-Korsakov at Heidelberg—a meeting which marked an epoch in his life. The older composer had much influence on the career of Stravinsky. Their views on music differed greatly, however.

Stravinsky worked hard. He attended concerts, visited museums and read widely. Rimsky-Korsakov, though alarmed at the revolutionary tendencies of his pupil, predicted for him great success. During the years 1905 and 1906 Stravinsky worked at orchestration. At this time his friends were members of the group surrounding Rimsky-Korsakov, including Glazounov and César-Cui.

On January 11, 1906, Stravinsky married. Soon after his marriage he finished a symphony which was performed in 1907 and was published later. Following this, in 1908, came his "Scherzo Fantastique," which was inspired by a reading of Maeterlinck's "Life of the Bee."

When Rimsky-Korsakov's daughter was married in 1908 Stravinsky sent his composition, "Fire Works," a symphonic fantasia, which, curiously, had been submitted for the approval of an English manufacturer of Chinese crackers. However, before the gift arrived by mail Rimsky-Korsakov died. As a tribute to his master's memory Stravinsky composed the Chant Funèbre.

In 1909 Stravinsky wrote "The Nightingale," a combination of opera and ballet, based on Hans Christian Andersen's fairy tale of the same name. This was produced in 1914.

Then came the discovery of Stravinsky by the director of the Russian ballet, Serge de Diaghileff. The young composer was commissioned to write a ballet on a Russian folk story, the scenario of which was furnished by Michel Fokine. Leon Bakst and Golovine, the scene painters, collaborated with him. This ballet, "The Fire Bird," was finished on May 18, 1910, and produced three weeks later. This production established Stravinsky's reputation in Paris.

The second of his ballets, "Petrouschka," was completed on May 26, 1911. It was first produced in Paris in the same year. The scene of Petrouschka is a carnival. One of the characters is a showman, and in his booth are three animated dolls. In the center is one with pink cheeks and a glassy stare. On one side of this is a fierce negro, and on the other the simple Petrouschka. These three play out a tragedy of love and jealousy, which ends with the shedding of Petrouschka's vital sawdust. One critic has said: "This ballet is, properly speaking, a travesty of human passion, expressed in terms of puppet gestures and illumined by music as expositor. The carnival music is a sheer joy, and the incidents making a demand upon music as a depictive medium have been treated not merely with marvelous skill, but with unfailing instinct for the true satirical touch. 'Petrouschka' is, in fact, the musical presentment of Russian fantastic humor in the second generation."

"The Crowning of Spring" was composed during the winter of 1912 and 1913, and was produced both in Paris and London during the following spring and summer.

Recently Stravinsky has composed several songs which are done in the same spirit as that in which he wrote his compositions for the orchestra.

PREPARED BY THE EDITORIAL STAFF OF THE MENTOR ASSOCIATION
ILLUSTRATION FOR THE MENTOR, VOL. 4, No. 18, SERIAL No. 118
COPYRIGHT, 1916, BY THE MENTOR ASSOCIATION, INC.

RUBINSTEIN
MOUSSORGSKY
TCHAIKOVSKY
RIMSKY-KORSAKOV
GLINKA
STRAVINSKY

So far as the world at large is concerned, Russian music—which has come so much to the fore in recent years—began with Rubinstein, who lived till 1894. There was, indeed, one other composer of note before him—Glinka—but Glinka's music, though very popular in Russia, remained almost unknown in other countries, whereas Rubinstein, and, after him, Tchaikovsky (also spelled Tschaikowsky), conquered the whole world.

Folk music, it is needless to say, flourished many centuries before Glinka. Folk tunes are like wild flowers, and in all countries the composers have heard the "call of the wild" and tried to woo these flowers and bring them to their gardens. This is particularly true of Russia, which has an abundance of folk songs that are unsurpassed in beauty and emotional appeal; indeed, Rubinstein and another eminent composer, César Cui (kwee), claim absolute supremacy for their country in the matter of national melodies. The tremendous size of the Empire, including, as it does, one-sixth of all the land on this globe, gives scope for an unparalleled variety of local color in songs, suggesting the great difference in costumes and customs. Asiatic traits are mingled with the European. Many of the songs are sad, as is to be expected in a populace often subjected to barbarian invasions, as well as to domestic tyranny; but perhaps an equal number are merry, with a gaiety as extravagant as the melancholy of the songs that are in the minor mode. As a rule, Russian peasants seem to prefer singing in groups to solo singing. There are many singing games; some of the current songs are of gypsy origin; and we find in the collections of Russian folk music (the best of which have been made by Balakiref and Rimsky-Korsakov) an endless variety, devoted to love, flattery, grief, war, religion, etc. Eugenie Lineff's "Peasant Songs of Great Russia" (transcribed from phonograms) gives interesting samples and descriptions. Lineff's choir has been heard in America.

SINGING AT AN OUTDOOR SHRINE

RUSSIAN PRIEST CHANTING

Russian Choirs and Basses

Church music is another branch of the divine art that flourished in Russia before the advent of the great composers. Five centuries ago the court at Moscow already had its church choir, and some of the Czars, including Ivan the Terrible, took a special interest in the musical service. Peter the Great had a private choir which he even took along on his travels.

In 1840, the French composer, Adolphe Charles Adam, on a visit to St. Petersburg (now Petrograd) found that church music was superior to any other kind in Russia. The choir of the Imperial Chapel sang without a conductor and without instrumental support, yet "with a justness of intonation of which one can have no idea."

A specialty of this choir, which gave it a "sense of peculiar strangeness," was the presence of bass voices that produced a marvelous effect by doubling the ordinary basses at the interval of an octave below them. These voices,

Adam continues, "if heard separately, would be intolerably heavy; when they are heard in the mass the effect is admirable." He was moved to tears by this choir, "stirred by such emotion as I had never felt before ... the most tremendous orchestra in the world could never give rise to this curious sensation, which was entirely different from any that I had supposed it possible for music to convey."

RUSSIAN ORGAN GRINDER

Similarly impressed was another French composer, Berlioz, when he heard the Imperial Choir sing a motet for eight voices: "Out of the web of harmonies formed by the incredibly intricate interlacing of the parts rose sighs and vague murmurs, such as one sometimes hears in dreams. From time to time came sounds so intense that they resembled human cries, which tortured the mind with the weight of sudden oppression and almost made the heart stop beating. Then the whole thing quieted down, diminishing with divinely slow graduations to a mere breath, as though a choir of angels was leaving the earth and gradually losing itself in the uttermost heights of heaven."

Italian and French Influences

Like all other European countries, Russia more than a century ago succumbed to the spell of Italian music. Young men were sent to Italy to study the art of song, while famous Italian singers and composers visited Russia and made the public familiar with their tuneful art. It was under the patronage of the Empress Anna that an Italian opera was for the first time performed in the Russian capital, in 1737. She was one of several rulers who deliberately fostered a love of art in the minds of their subjects. Under the Empress Elizabeth music became "a fashionable craze," and "every great landowner started his private band or choir." Russia became what it still is—

the place where (except in America) traveling artists could reap their richest harvests.

PLAYER OF REED PIPE

The high salaries paid tempted some of the leading Italian composers, such as Cimarosa (Cheemahrosah), Sarti, and Paisiello (Paheeseello), to make their home for years in Russia, where they composed and produced their operas. Near the end of the eighteenth century French influences also asserted themselves, but the Italians continued to predominate, so that when the Russians themselves—in the reign of Catherine the Great (1761-1796)—took courage and began to compose operas, Italian tunefulness and methods were conspicuous features of them.

Glinka, the Pioneer

The operas of Glinka, as well as those of Rubinstein and Tchaikovsky, betrayed the influence of Italy on Russian music. Though not the first Russian opera composer, Michal Ivanovich Glinka is the first of historic note. Rubinstein goes so far as to claim for him a place among the greatest five of all composers (the others being, in his opinion, Bach, Beethoven, Schubert and Chopin), but this is a ludicrously patriotic exaggeration. His master work is "A Life for the Czar," which created a new epoch in Russian music. The hero of the plot is a peasant, Soussanin, who, during a war between Poland and Russia, is pressed into service as a guide by a Polish army corps. He saves the Czar by misleading the Poles, and falls a victim to their vengeance. In his autobiography Glinka says: "The scene where Soussanin leads the Poles astray in the forest I read aloud while composing, and entered so completely into the situation of my hero that I used to feel my hair standing on end and cold shivers down my back." It is under such conditions that

24

master works are created.

ROMANTIC DANCE

A MOUJIK (PEASANT) DANCE

Although following the conventional Italian forms, "A Life for the Czar" is in most respects thoroughly Slavic—partly Russian, partly Polish. While composing the score he followed the plan of using the national music of Poland and Russia to contrast the two countries. In some cases he used actual folk tunes, including one he overheard a cab driver sing. In other instances he invented his own melodies, but dyed them in the national colors. As the eminent French composer, Alfred Bruneau (bree´-no), remarked, "by means of a harmony or a simple orchestral touch," Glinka "could give an air which is apparently as Italian as possiblea penetrating perfume of Russian nationality."

By his utilizing of folk tunes in building up works of art—he did the same thing in his next opera, "Ruslan and Ludmilla"—Glinka entered a path on which most of the Russian composers of his time, and later on, followed his lead; but his influence did not stop there. He was also the pioneer who opened up the road into the dense jungle of discords, unusual scales, and odd rhythms, which have made much of the music by later Russian composers seem as if written according to a new grammar. Furthermore, Rosa Newmarch, who is the best historian in English of Russian opera, writes that "it is impossible not to realize that the fantastic Russian ballets of the present day owe much to Glinka's first introduction of Eastern dances into 'Ruslan and Ludmilla'."

MICHAL GLINKA

Clearly, Glinka was the father of Russian opera. He wrote some good concert pieces, too.

Rubinstein, the Russian Mendelssohn

Anton Rubinstein is considered to have been, next to Franz Liszt, the greatest pianist the world has ever heard. His technical execution was not flawless, but no one paid any attention to that, because of the overwhelming grandeur and emotional sweep of his playing. Like Liszt, however, he tired of the laurels of a performer, his ambition being to become the Russian Beethoven. He got no higher, however, than the level of Mendelssohn. Both Mendelssohn and Rubinstein were for years extremely popular. If they are less so today, that is owing to the superficial character of much of their music. Yet both were great geniuses; in their master works they reached the high water mark of musical creativeness. Rubinstein is at his best in his "Ocean" symphony, his Persian songs, some of his chamber works for stringed instruments, alone or with piano, two of his concertos for piano and orchestra, and his pieces for piano alone, the number of which is 238. Among these there are gems of the first water.

PEASANT WITH ACCORDION

A Rubinstein revival is much to be desired in these days, when so few composers are able to create new melodies. When it comes, in response to the demands of audiences, which are very partial to this composer, at least three of his nineteen operas will be revived: "The Demon," "Nero," and "The Maccabees." Opera goers love, above all things, melody, and Rubinstein's operas, like his concert pieces, are full of it. He was himself to blame for the failure of most of his operas, for he stubbornly refused to swim with the Wagnerian current, which swept everything before it. He hated Wagner intensely, yet he might have learned from him the art of writing music dramas of permanent value.

Five of his operas are on Biblical subjects. They are really oratorios with scenery, action and costumes. He dreamed of erecting a special theater somewhere for the production of these "sacred operas," as Wagner did for his music dramas at Bayreuth; but nothing came of this plan, and he became more and more embittered as he grew older, because so many of his schemes failed.

Apart from their abundant melody there is nothing in Rubinstein's best works that fascinates us more than the exhibits of glowing Oriental and Hebrew "coloring"—as we call it for want of a better word. He also made excellent use of national Russian melodies, though not nearly to the same extent as Glinka and his followers, the "nationalists." Before considering them it will be advisable to speak of the greatest of all the Russian composers.

MUSIC AMONG THE LOWLY

Tchaikovsky, the Melancholy

It is commonly believed that in music the public wants something "quick and devilish"; but this is far from the truth. For social, political, and especially climatic reasons, the Russians, with their long and dreary winters, are supposed to be a melancholy nation. The most melancholy of their composers is Peter Ilich Tchaikovsky, and of his works the most popular by far, throughout the world, is the most lugubrious of them all, the heart rending "Pathetic Symphony," which is today second in popularity to no other orchestral work of any country. "All hope abandon, ye who enter here," might well be its motto. More than any funeral march ever composed, it embodies, in the *adagio lamentoso*, which ends it, the concentrated quintessence of despair, "the luxury of woe." It was Tchaikovsky's symphonic swan song. At the time of his death there was a rumor that he had written it deliberately as his own dirge before committing suicide; but it is now known that he died of cholera.

What endears the "Pathetic Symphony" to such a multitude of music lovers is, furthermore, its abundance of soulful melody. This abundance characterizes many of his other compositions. Indeed, so conspicuous, so ingratiating, is the flow of melody in his works, that one might think he was one of those Italian masters who made their home in Russia. It must be borne in mind, however, that the Italians have not a monopoly of melodists—think of the Austrians, Haydn, Mozart (who was the idol of Tchaikovsky's youth) and Schubert; the Germans, Bach, Beethoven, Schumann, Wagner; the Frenchmen, Bizet and Gounod; the Norwegian, Grieg; the Pole, Chopin. With them as a melodist ranks Tchaikovsky, and this is the highest praise that could be bestowed on him. The charm of original melody gives distinction to his songs, the best of which are the "Spanish Serenade," "None but a Lonely Heart," and "Why So Pale Are the Roses?"

STREET MUSICIANS

THE MUSIC LESSON

There is less of it in his piano pieces, but his first concerto for piano and orchestra, and his violin concerto, have an abundance of it and are therefore popular favorites—as much as his "Slavic March," his "1812" overture, and his "Nut Cracker Suite," which is also full of quaint humor, and which had the distinction of introducing a new instrument now much used in orchestras—

the "celesta"—a small keyboard instrument, the hammers of which strike thin plates of steel, producing silvery bell-like tones. This suite consists of pieces taken from his ballet of the same name.

Among his stage works are eight operas, only two of which, "Eugene Onegin" and "The Queen of Spades," have, however, been successful outside of Russia; but in Russia the first named has long been second in popularity only to "A Life for the Czar."

Moussorgsky and Musical Nihilism

MODESTE PETROVICH MOUSSORGSKY

One of the works most frequently performed at the Metropolitan Opera House in New York during the last three seasons has been the "Boris Godounov" of Modeste Petrovich Moussorgsky. It is concerned with one of the most tragic incidents in the history of Russia. Boris Godounov usurps the imperial crown after assassinating the Czar's younger brother, Dimitri. After he has ruled some years, he is driven to insanity by the appearance of a young monk who pretends to be Dimitri, rescued at the last moment and brought up in a monastery. In setting this plot to music Moussorgsky adopted the principles of musical "nihilism," which consisted in deliberately disregarding the established operatic order of things. The musical interest centers chiefly in the choruses, leaving little for the soloists, apart from dramatic action. Moussorgsky not only liked what was "coarse, unpolished and ugly," as Tchaikovsky put it, but he refused to submit to the necessary discipline of musical training, the result being that not only "Boris Godounov," but his next opera, "Kovanstchina," could not be staged successfully until Rimsky-Korsakov had thoroughly revised them, especially in regard to harmonic treatment and orchestration. The charm of "Boris" lies in the pictures it presents of Russian life, and its echoes of folk music.

PEASANTS IN MOSCOW
Listening to public band concert

Of the songs by its composer few have become known outside of Russia. Some are satirical—he has been called the "Juvenal of musicians"—and it has been said of his lyrics in general that "had the realistic schools of painting and fiction never come into being we might still construct from Moussorgsky's songs the whole psychology of Russian life."

Rimsky-Korsakov and the Nationalists

Moussorgsky and the man who helped to make his inspired but ungrammatical works presentable to the world—Nicholas Andreievich Rimsky-Korsakov—belonged to a coterie of composers known as the nationalists. The other three were Balakiref, whose output as a composer was small, but whose two collections of Russian folk tunes are considered the best in existence; Borodin, who is best known in this country through an orchestral piece called "In the Steppes of Central Asia" and his "Prince Igor," which has been produced at the Metropolitan Opera House, and César Cui, who is more interesting as a writer than as a composer. He has well set forth the tenets of the "nationalists," chief of which is that a composer cannot be a truly patriotic Russian master unless he uses folk tunes as the bricks for building up his works.

MILI BALAKIREF   RIMSKY-KORSAKOV

ALEXANDER P. BORODIN

Because Rubinstein and Tchaikovsky did not do this to any extent these nationalists looked down on them, and decried them as cosmopolitans—belonging to the world rather than to Russia. Rubinstein, who had a caustic pen, retorted by declaring that the nationalists borrowed folk tunes because they were unable to invent good melodies of their own. To a certain extent this was true, but it does not apply to Rimsky-Korsakov, who is, next to Rubinstein and Tchaikovsky, the greatest of the Russian melodists and composers. Theodore Thomas considered him the greatest of them all. With this opinion few will agree, but no one can fail to admire the glowing colors of his orchestral works, the greatest of which is "Scheherazade," which is based on "The Arabian Nights," and is concerned with Sinbad's vessel and Bagdad. Of his dozen or more operas none has become acclimated outside of Russia. As a teacher he might be called the Russian Liszt, because not a few of his pupils acquired national and international fame; among them Glazounov, Liadov, Arensky, Ippolitov-Ivanov, Gretchaninov, Taneiev (tah-nay-ev) and Stravinsky.

Stravinsky and the Russian Ballet

Four of the most prominent Russian composers have visited America: Rubinstein, Tchaikovsky, Rachmaninov and Scriabin. Rachmaninov, the only one of the four still living, owed the beginning of his international fame to the great charm of his preludes for piano. Scriabin was one of the musical "anarchists" who now abound in Europe—composers who try to be "different" at any cost of law, order, tradition and beauty. One of his quaint conceits was an attempt to combine perfume and colored lights with orchestral sounds. Musical frightfulness is rampant in some of his symphonies, in which horrible dissonances clash fiercely and "without warning."

ALEXANDER GLAZOUNOV   ALEXANDER SCRIABIN

The latest of the Russians who has come to the fore—Igor Stravinsky— also revels in dissonances, but in his case they are not only excusable but even fascinating, because there is a reason behind them. He uses them to illustrate and emphasize humorous, grotesque or fantastic plots and details, such as are presented in his pantomimic ballets, "Petrouschka," and "The Fire Bird." There is an entirely new musical "atmosphere" in these two works, and the public, as well as the critics, have taken to them as ducks do to water. If the Diaghileff Ballet Russe which toured the United States last season had done nothing but produce these two entertainments, it would have been worth their while to cross the Atlantic. They have made the world acquainted with a Russian who may appeal, in his way, as strongly as Rubinstein and Tchaikovsky. His latest efforts are reported to be in the direction of the cult of ugliness for its own sake. But perhaps he will get over that—or, maybe some of us will come to like ugliness in music as we do in bulldogs. Opinions as to what is ugly or beautiful in music have changed frequently.

CÉSAR A. CUI   SERGEI RACHMANINOV

The Character of Russian Music

The musical character of the great masters is unmistakable. When an expert hears a piece by a famous composer for the first time he can usually guess who wrote it. But when it comes to judging the *national* source of an unfamiliar piece, the problem is puzzling. It is true that Italian music usually betrays its country. Widely as Verdi and Puccini differ from Rossini and Donizetti, they have unmistakable traits in common. The same cannot be said of the French masters, or the German. Gounod and Berlioz, both French composers, are as widely apart as the poles. Flotow, who composed "Martha," was a German, but his opera is as utterly unlike Wagner's "Tristan and Isolde" as two things can be.

The question, "What are the characteristics of Russian music?" is, for similar reasons, difficult to answer. As in other countries, there are as many styles of music as there are great composers. Moreover, Rubinstein is less like any other Russian than he is like the German Mendelssohn. If a "composite portrait" could be made of the works of prominent Russian composers, it might, nevertheless, give some idea of their general characteristics. Tchaikovsky's passionate melody, reinforced by inspired passages from Rimsky-Korsakov and by the tuneful strains of Rubinstein, would give prominence to what is best in Russian music. A more distinct race trait is the partiality of Russian masters for deeply despondent strains, alternating with fierce outbursts of unrestrained hilarity, clothed in garish, barbaric orchestral colors. In startling contrast with the alluring charms of Rubinstein's Oriental and Semitic traits are the harsh dissonances of Moussorgsky, Scriabin, and Stravinsky. Blending all these traits in our composite musical portrait, with a rich infusion of folk-songs of diverse types, both Asiatic and European, we glimpse the main characteristics of Russian music.

MAKERS OF THE RUSSIAN BALLET

From left to right—Leonide Massine, dancer; Leon Bakst, costume and scene designer, and Igor Stravinsky, composer

SUPPLEMENTARY READING

A SHORT HISTORY OF RUSSIAN MUSIC   *By Arthur Pougin*

THE RUSSIAN OPERA   *By Rosa Newmarch*
THE LIFE AND LETTERS OF TCHAIKOVSKY *By Modeste Tchaikovsky*
ANTON RUBINSTEIN'S AUTOBIOGRAPHY
PEASANT SONGS OF GREAT RUSSIA   *By Eugenie Lineff*
A HISTORY OF RUSSIAN MUSIC   *By M. Montagu-Nathan*

THE OPEN LETTER

RUSSIAN BALLET

A scene from "Soleil de Nuit," one of Serge de Diaghileff's ballets. The ballet was arranged by Massine, who occupies the center of the group. The music is by Rimsky-Korsakov, and the scenery and costumes were designed by Leon Bakst's favorite pupil, M. Larionoff

Russian composers of our time are in luck. A wealthy timber merchant named Balaiev (bah-lah-ee-ev) appointed himself their special patron a number of years ago. In 1885 he founded a publishing house at Leipzig, and spent large sums of money printing the works of Russian composers and financing productions of Russian music all over the world.

✱ ✱ ✱

In America the missionary work has been carried on in a number of ways. Rubinstein toured the States in 1872, and gave 215 concerts, which created a tremendous sensation and drew attention to Russian compositions. Tchaikovsky visited America as the special guest of the festival given in celebration of the opening of Carnegie Music Hall in 1891, and during his visit, many pieces of Russian music were performed. Slivinsky, the pianist, made a tour of America, and Chaliapin, the celebrated Russian bass, appeared for one season at the Metropolitan Opera House. For several years the oldest orchestra of America, the New York Philharmonic, had for its conductor one of Russia's leading musicians, Wassilly Safonoff, who frequently introduced novelties from Russia into his programs. On a larger scale, Russian standard works have been performed in New York City and on tour in America, by the Russian Symphony Orchestra, which was founded in 1893 and conducted by Modest Altschuler.

✱ ✱ ✱

During the 90's, Mme. Lineff brought over the large Russian choir that made Americans acquainted with their peasant songs and their unique way of singing them. Then came the Balalaika Orchestra. The Balalaika is the Czar's favorite instrument, and the Imperial Balalaika Band, which came to the United States by the Czar's permission, devoted itself largely to Russian folk music. Several of the numbers played, especially the "Song of the Volga Bargemen," made a sensational success in concert. The Balalaika is used to accompany folk songs in the manner of a guitar, but the Balalaika has a triangular body and only three strings, which are made to vibrate like those of a mandolin.

And now we have the Russian Ballet, made familiar to the American public by the famous dancer Pavlowa, and, within the last year, by the Diaghileff Ballet Company, of which the leading spirits are Stravinsky, the composer; Leon Bakst, the master designer, and Massine, the accomplished actor-dancer. Surely the day of Russian music has come.

EDITOR

W. D. Moffat
EDITOR

CPSIA information can be obtained
at www.ICGtesting.com
Printed in the USA
LVHW111220110820
662878LV00007B/959